One Is A Warrior

One Is A Warrior

A Lawson Holland Novella

M.P. MacDougall

DYSFUNCTIONAL DOZEN PRESS
Subsidiary of
DTwelve Media, LLC

One Is A Warrior

For information, inquiries, or updates on new editions, contact: mp@mpmacdougall.com

ISBN: 978-1-962138-16-1

For the Warriors, who have what it takes to bring the rest of us back.

Out of every one hundred men, ten shouldn't even be there, eighty are just targets, nine are the real fighters, and we are lucky to have them, for they make the battle.

Ah, but the one; one is a warrior, and he will bring the others back.

- Unknown

CHAPTER ONE

Little Creek

Little Creek, Virginia
June 1989

Lawson Holland followed the team leader into the squad bay and looked around. Several men looked up from where they were seated around the room. Holland didn't quite know what to expect on this, his first day with his SEAL Team. He'd just come from the hell of the Navy's BUD/S qualification course, followed by an intensive sniper school - and he still wasn't fully qualified to be called a Navy SEAL.

He was in a weird sort of limbo that he didn't yet fully understand. The next several months would be spent training and working with his assigned SEAL team, but he still wasn't quite one of them. More than anything, he didn't want to make a bad first impression.

"Listen up!" The team leader, Lieutenant Flaherty, barked at the lounging men. "New guy." He jerked a thumb at Holland. "This is Lawson Holland, just in from sniper school. Make him feel welcome." Flaherty turned to go, but leaned close to

Holland's ear as he left him. "Welcome to Little Creek."

"Thank you, sir."

Flaherty stiffened and gave Holland a sideways look. "Do me a favor. Don't call me 'sir' unless you're asking to date my daughter, got it?" Several of the men snickered. Flaherty was closer to five feet tall than he was to six, and he had a baby face that made him look like he was barely old enough to shave. The idea that he'd have a dating-age daughter was plainly ludicrous.

"Yes, si-" Holland caught himself. "Got it."

Flaherty grinned. "Quick learner. I'll leave you to it, then." He looked around the room. "You boys play nice, now."

Holland watched him go, then turned back to face the room - which had gone totally silent.

One man at the far end of the room looked up from the rifle he was assembling. "So? Tell us about yourself, Meat."

Holland cleared his throat. "Well, I -"

The room erupted in catcalls and jeers.

"Shut yer pie hole!"

"Nobody cares!"

"Who asked you?"

Holland flushed slightly, not sure what to do.

The first man stood. "Knock it off, ya chuckleheads." He looked at Holland. "Seriously. Go ahead and tell us about yourself. We're not gonna bite ya."

Holland watched him for a moment. "All right. I -"

"Stow that noise!"

"Sit down!"

"Oxygen thief! Stop wasting our air!"

This time the shouting was punctuated by a flurry of thrown objects ranging from dirty socks to wadded up candy wrappers and empty soda cans. Holland held an arm over his face and turned slightly to avoid the worst of it. Now he was smiling, realizing they would probably happily carry on the game as long as he continued to fall for it.

"So?" A wiry man on the right side of the room said when the rest of them had settled down. He had a name tag pinned to his shoulder that said 'Hello! My name is Lance. How may I help?' He waved a beckoning hand at Holland. "Why don't you tell us about yourself?"

Holland just shrugged and smiled. The first man who had spoken to him crossed the room and stuck out his hand. "Boone MacAulay. Nice to meet ya, Meat."

A man with dark hair sticking out from beneath a battered Dallas Cowboys hat spoke up. "Don't listen to him, Meat! His name is Ballroom!"

Holland glanced at the man, then back to MacAulay. He decided not to push his luck. "Lawson Holland. Likewise, Boone."

"What's a Lawman Holler?" the wiry man wanted to know.

One of his buddies picked up the cue. "No, no. He said his name was 'Unlawful Halter.'"

"You're way off," another man said. "It's 'Long Haul Sunshine.'"

"He said he was lost in Holland," a fourth man replied. "Easy enough to do. Place is flatter'n a pancake. Can't get yer bearings. Don't feel too bad about it, though, Meat. We'll teach you how to navigate."

"Y'all got wax in your ears!" a fifth SEAL shouted from the back of the room. "He said, 'Floss on Holidays'!" This was met with another wave of jeers, the loudest speculating that the man who delivered that particular insult wouldn't know dental floss if he was being strangled with it.

"TULIP!" Boone's voice boomed suddenly. The rest of the men stopped talking.

Holland looked at him with his brow furrowed and eyes pleading. *"Tulip?"*

Boone grinned. "On account of 'em growing so many tulips in Holland." He paused, then raised his eyebrows. "Your name's Holland? Get it?"

Holland nodded in resignation. "Got it. Makes perfect sense."

"Good," Boone said, his grin getting wider. "Let's get ya squared away, *Tulip*."

For the remainder of that summer, Holland lived, worked and trained alongside his new team. He got to know each of the men, and found that he liked them all. They were an odd group - nothing like what he'd imagined when he had signed up for SEAL tryouts the previous year. Misled by movies and rumors, he'd half expected to be surrounded by muscle-bound supermen, but the reality was that these SEALs looked pretty much like everybody else. True, they were all in phenomenal physical shape, but none of them were hugely muscular. They were mostly lean, well built, athletic men who looked as though they could run fifty miles before breakfast without breaking much of a sweat.

And most of them probably could.

They trained together on firearms, explosives, hand to hand combat, building assaults, vehicle takedowns - anything and everything that could possibly be of use in a combat situation - they found ways to train for it. It was exhausting, but the constant good humor of his teammates made it seem easier. The men joked about *everything*. And while they trained with an almost obsessive intensity, picking apart each other's mistakes and re-working problems until they found solutions, they also found creative ways to avoid the most onerous exercises.

Every Tuesday morning, regardless of the weather, they would have to swim two miles in the waters of Chesapeake Bay. A bus would transport them all to a drop-off point near the Lesner Bridge on highway 60, and they would all pile out, dressed in wet suits and swim fins, and plunge into the icy water for the swim paralleling the beach back to the Chesapeake Bay Bridge, where the bus would pick them up again. Sometimes the men would deliberately schedule other appointments on Tuesdays to avoid the hated swim. Other methods were more creative. One man crawled out of the rear emergency exit when the bus stopped at a light on the way to the drop-off point. He calmly strode across two lanes of traffic, jumped a fence, and ran through a subdivision to the beach, cutting his swim distance in half.

Another team member waited for Lieutenant Flaherty to leave the team's ready room with his gear, then crawled into Flaherty's gear cage and went to sleep under a pile of equipment. Later, when he heard the bus pull up outside, he dashed from the cage and into the shower, emerging dripping wet in his wetsuit as the rest of the team walked in. "Great swim, today, boys!" he bellowed. Nobody bought it. Flaherty looked at the mess of scattered gear bags on the floor of his gear cage and just shook his head.

As much as they hated the weekly swim, they all loved weapons training of any kind. Once during a training evolution on explosives, Boone looked up from the detonator he was holding long enough to tell Holland, "We get paid to blow stuff up and kill people, kid. Best gig in the world!"

Then he punched the button, and a wrecked car five hundred yards downrange leaped into the air on a column of smoke and fire. The loud crack of the detonation and the shock wave reached them a heartbeat later.

"Except," Louie, the Range Control Officer, said. "Except, we don't ever *really* get to kill anybody. So mostly, we compensate for that by blowing *more* stuff up." He thumbed the button on his own detonator, and another junkyard castoff cartwheeled into the air.

It was a running joke around the team - as well as a sore spot - that the SEALs were under-utilized. They trained harder and more often on more specialties than any other unit in the military, but they hadn't been deployed on a real world contingency since the invasion of Grenada six years earlier. Most of the guys on Holland's team hadn't even been in the military back then, much less been on a SEAL team.

Boone had joined the teams four years before Holland. He was *very* good at just about everything, but the fact was, he had never fired a single shot at another human in combat. It bothered him, and it bothered every other man on the team. It wasn't that they were a pack of bloodthirsty killers - it was just that they often spent up to sixteen hours a day training so hard for the real thing that their training was more grueling and dangerous than most people's reality. They had a natural desire to use that training, but no real mission that required it.

Holland had been with the team for just two weeks when he was notified that he had a school date for his final SEAL tactical qualification course. He would be away from the team for thirteen weeks, on an intensive regimen of advanced tactics covering everything he'd learned to that point, and then some. Boone was watching him pack his bags in the ready room the night before he was supposed to ship out to the Caribbean for combat diving qualification.

Boone leaned against the gear cage with his arms folded as Holland stuffed a bag with clothes and gear. "Don't forget your favorite blanky," he quipped.

Holland grinned. He'd gotten accustomed to Boone's near-constant jokes and teasing. "You sure you won't miss it? I don't really need it any more."

Boone chuckled. "That's not what your Mom told me."

Holland looked up, suddenly glaring. "That's not cool, man. My mom died three months ago."

Boone's face fell. "Aw, man, I'm sorry - it was just a joke… aw, crap."

Holland tried to stifle his grin, and failed. "Gotcha."

"Ohhh," Boone relaxed and shook his head. "That's cold, brother."

Holland laughed and went back to stuffing his bag. "Why 'Ballroom'?"

"That's gotta be a new record," Boone said.

"What do you mean?"

"Most everybody I meet asks me that question inside of five minutes of being introduced. You? You don't say anything for two weeks, then you drop it in outta nowhere."

"I'm cultivating an air of mystery," Holland said. "So? Why 'Ballroom'?"

"Not the most manly callsign for a manly man like me, is that what you're thinking?"

"Yeah, that," Holland said. "Except for the 'manly man' part."

"Funny. Well, seeing as how you're on your way to serve your country by gloriously drowning in training, I guess I can tell you. When I was a clueless piece of new meat, much like yourself, I made the unforgivable mistake of telling some yahoo that my parents made me take dance lessons when I was a teenager."

Holland barked out a laugh, but choked it back when he saw Boone scowling. "No kidding?"

"No kidding. Ballroom dance lessons - hence the snappy moniker."

"Oh, man…"

"Yeah, go ahead and laugh," Boone said. "But lemme ask you this - do you have any idea how many girls you can meet when you're the only dude in an entire dance class?"

"'Ballroom' is sounding more manly by the minute," Holland laughed. He zipped the duffel closed and stood up. "All set. I hope."

Boone grabbed the bag. "Let's get you to the airport, then." Holland fell in step next to him as they headed out the door. "So, you sure your mom's not really dead?"

"Pretty sure," Holland said. "She's a hundred and five, but she's still pretty spry. Takes ballroom dancing classes at the senior center twice a week."

"You're hilarious."

CHAPTER TWO

Jamaica

Port Royal, Jamaica
September 1989

Holland straddled the bar stool and leaned back with his elbows on the bar, a bottle of Red Stripe Jamaican beer dangling from his right hand. He stared out at the ocean, not twenty yards from where he sat, and smiled. He still found it hard to believe that he was here, sitting at a beach bar, watching the morning waves in a tropical paradise, because of his *job*. He chuckled.

"Something's funny, you should share, yeah?"

Holland turned around, startled. He hadn't realized that he'd laughed out loud. Standing behind the bar was a beautiful young Jamaican woman, idly wiping a glass with a towel while nearly blinding him with her smile. He tried to smile back, but found he'd suddenly forgotten how to control his face.

The woman furrowed her brow slightly. "I hope it wasn't *me* that was funny, now?"

"Um, ah, no," Holland stammered. "You're not funny, uh…"

She stopped wiping the glass, and her eyebrows went up a notch.

"No, no," he waved his free hand, as if he was trying to put out a small fire in the air. "I meant to say, I wasn't laughing at you."

She smiled. "Well, that's a comfort." She went back to cleaning glasses. "So why are you all alone, laughing at yourself? Where are your buddies?"

Holland couldn't take his eyes off of hers. "My buddies, ma'am? How do you know I'm not here alone?"

"It's hard to miss. You're one of those SEALs, yeah?"

"What makes you say that? I don't think you and I have met before now, have we?" he looked around behind the bar. "By the way, where'd the other guy go?"

"My brother? He has two little babies at home. Sometimes I come in early and help out with the bar, so he can go home and play with his little ones."

Holland nodded. "Oh. Well, the way you snuck up on me, *you* might as well be a SEAL, and I can stay here and help your brother with the bar."

She laughed. Holland thought it was about the nicest sound he'd ever heard.

She glanced at the bottle in his hand. "You want another?"

"Sure, that'd be great." He'd only planned on having one beer after coming in from a five mile run on the beach. Now he had no idea *what* he was planning - he suddenly didn't want to leave the bar. If she'd offered him a bottle of motor oil to drink, he probably would have gladly accepted it, just so he'd have a reason to stay. He watched her as she dug in a cooler behind the bar and came up with a dark bottle.

"You look like you need something different," she said, sliding the bottle across the bar. He picked it up and looked at the label. It read *Dragon Stout* in bold letters above a writhing red dragon.

"Stout? I don't think I've ever had that."

"Think of it as Red Stripe's older, darker brother." She flashed that smile again, with a hint of mischief this time. "Not afraid of the dark, are you?"

Holland was suddenly aware that he was staring at her, half slack-jawed at her double entendre and unable to form a coherent reply. "Uh… I… Uhh…"

Now she *really* laughed. "Your ears are red!"

He reached a tentative hand up and touched his right ear. "Must be a sunburn." With an effort, he finally looked away from her smile, feigning interest in his bottle of stout. He couldn't stop smiling, in spite of his sudden nervousness.

"So, should I call you Mr. SEAL, or do you have a real name?"

He looked up, finally remembering his manners. "I'm Lawson," he said, offering his hand. "Lawson Holland."

She tilted her head slightly. "That doesn't sound like a made-up name. You could almost pass for a Jamaican with a name like that." She shook his hand. "Alexandra Sinclair. But everybody calls me Alex."

"Nice to meet you, Alex." He forced himself to let go of her hand. "What do you mean, my name doesn't sound made up?"

"You're not the first SEAL to come into this bar," she said, going back to wiping glasses. "You might be the first shy one, though." Holland felt his face redden again as she went on. "Most of them think they're clever - they try to impress me and the other girls. Some of the worst pick-up lines you ever heard. And they give fake names. I think they think it'll be easier to disappear later if we don't know who they really are. Do you know who came in here last week and tried to pick me up?"

"Who?"

"George Bush."

Holland shook his head. "The *President of the United States* tried to pick you up?"

"He tried, but his friend kept trying to impress me at the same time. Neither of them realized they were wasting their time, because I don't date tourists. They ended up rolling around in the sand and swearing at each other for nothing."

Holland laughed. "So what happened then?"

"They both left, but President Bush's friend came back twenty minutes later and tried again. Do you know what his 'name' was?"

"Let me guess," Holland said. "Ronald Reagan?"

Alex smiled again. "I think I'm the only girl in Jamaica who's been fought over by two American presidents!"

"I think I know those guys," Holland said. "I'm really sorry about that."

She waved a dismissive hand. "They were harmless. At least, they were harmless to me. I think Mr. Reagan might have broken Mr. Bush's nose."

Now it was Holland's turn to laugh. "I *definitely* know those guys!"

"So," Alex said. "Why haven't I seen you before? You don't like the beach party scene?"

Holland shook his head. "Not much, no. Too many drunks come out at night. I like the beach, though, so I come down and run in the mornings. This is my first time on this stretch of beach since I got here." He gave her a sidelong glance. "It's nice."

Again, she flashed her blinding smile. "Well, I'm glad you like it, Lawson."

Holland talked with Alex for another half hour before some more early risers trailed into the bar and interrupted them. He didn't want to leave, but as business in the bar started to pick up, she had to focus more on the other customers. He fished out some cash to pay his tab.

"Thanks for the stout," he told her. "I think I like it better than regular beer."

"My pleasure," she said as she opened the register to get his change.

He waved her off. "Keep it, please. I appreciate the conversation."

She smiled again, her eyes flashing. "I enjoyed meeting you, Lawson. Will you run on the beach here again tomorrow?"

"I think I might," he said, pulling his battered ball cap onto his head. "Why do you ask?"

"No reason." She poured a cup of coffee for another man further down the bar who looked almost ready to fall off his stool. "I might just give my brother another day off, though."

"Your brother's a lucky man," Holland said. "I hope to see you then." He turned to go, then said over his shoulder, "In the meantime, watch out for stray presidents."

"I'll do that," Alex said with a laugh. Further down the bar, the man with the coffee slowly fell off his stool with a thump.

At sunset three days later, Holland and Alex walked together along the beach. Holland's combat diving course had ended that afternoon, and he was scheduled to fly back to Virginia in the morning. He and Alex had spent almost every spare minute together since they'd met, just walking the beach and talking, or sharing a meal, laughing at Holland's awkward shyness or Alex's tendency to spill anything within reach.

It had been the best three days of Holland's life.

But now, it came to the point. He was leaving in the morning, headed back to a job that would keep him deployed or training more than ten months in every year. If a real world situation did come up, he had no illusions about his own invincibility. More than anything, he knew it wasn't the sort of life that someone like Alex deserved. He walked in silence, angry with himself that he was going to have to walk away. And he hadn't even so much as held her hand.

Alex glanced at him out of the corner of her eye. "You're very quiet."

"Sorry." He looked south across the narrow channel at Rackham's Cay, where they'd kayaked together the previous day. Alex had been thrilled to show him around her hometown, and he'd been just as happy to let her. He thought he was probably being ridiculous - he'd only known her for a couple of days, so why was he so reluctant to leave?

"Is something wrong?"

He looked at her. "No. I'm just sorta kicking myself, that's all."

"Sounds uncomfortable." She grinned.

"I guess so. Look, I want to thank you for spending so much of your time with me the past few days. I, uh... I'm wishing I didn't have to go, now."

She smiled again. "Why would you want to stay?"

"Well, I'd like to spend more time... exploring the island. With you." His heart was hammering.

She turned and looked across the water. "That would be nice, but you know I don't date tourists."

Holland laughed. "Good thing I'm down here on business then, huh?"

"Good thing." Her smile faded slightly. "Can I ask something?"

"Sure. Fire away."

"You're not normal."

"That's not really a question."

"No - let me finish. You're not like the average single guy on vacation here. They're usually rude, sometimes downright vulgar. But the entire time we've spent together, you've been a perfect gentleman. You're polite, you're respectful, and you haven't tried anything at all with me. I'm just curious - why not?"

Holland cleared his throat, then shuffled a toe in the sand. "It's not for a lack of wanting to, that's for sure."

She dropped her head lower, trying to see his expression. "Then what is it?"

Suddenly the words flooded out of him. "I didn't want to disrespect you, Lexie. You're an amazing person, and I didn't come down here expecting to meet anybody, and then I met you, but I didn't want to try to force something to happen in just a couple of days, because I think you deserve so much better than that. But now it's almost time for me to go, and I'm kicking myself for not saying something earlier, and -"

"You called me Lexie." Her voice was suddenly very quiet.

"I did? I'm sorry - I didn't even realize - it just came out that way..."

She put her hand in his. "No, I like it. My grandfather used to call me that when I was a little girl."

Holland was looking down at their interlaced fingers, marveling at how perfectly her hand fit in his. "I just don't see how this is going to work out. I mean, I'm never home. My job is dangerous, and there're more failed marriages among the SEALs than any other units in the military."

"Are you asking me to marry you?" She was grinning broadly at his discomfort, but her eyes were shining.

"What? No... I mean, not yet... I mean... Dangit, I'm not sure what I mean. What I'm saying is I think you can do better than settling for someone who'll be gone more than he's there, and someday might never come home at all."

"You want to know what I think?"

He let out a long breath, grateful not to have to explain himself further. "Sure."

"I think you're not very good at romance."

"I won't argue with that."

"But I think I don't care much about romance, anyway."

"You don't?"

"No. It's overrated." She went up on her toes and kissed his cheek. "But still, you worry too much. We don't have to talk about weddings right now. You can write, can't you?"

He was staring at her. "Yeah, I can write. It's harder to put your foot in your mouth on paper."

"Good. We can write each other letters when you get back to the states. You can practice your romance skills, and I can decide if I *really* want to be with somebody like you."

CHAPTER THREE

Preparations

Little Creek, Virginia
  October 1989

"She said she didn't care about romance?" Boone was sitting on a stool in his gear cage, scribbling notes about their latest close quarters assault drill.

"That's what she said." Holland had been back in Little Creek for three weeks, and had managed to write Lexie almost every day. He was working on his latest letter as they spoke.

"Yeah, she lied," Boone said.

Holland grinned, but kept writing.

Boone looked across the aisle at him. "You hear me? I said, she lied. There isn't a woman alive that doesn't want romance. Trust me."

"Because you're so romantic yourself?"

"Damn straight. I'm a regular Casablanca."

"Casanova."

"That's what I said, don't try to change the subject. Writing all those letters isn't gonna cut it, brother. You're gonna have to fly down there, surprise her, sweep her off her feet. All that kinda crap."

"You're making me feel all fluttery inside," Holland said. "You been watching soap operas again, haven't you?"

"Listen up!" Lieutenant Flaherty came into the team room, interrupting them before Boone could answer. Boone just gave Holland a knowing wink and nod as Flaherty continued. "I have an announcement to make. It looks like we might be going downrange finally. Command is working on several contingencies for an operation to take out Manuel Noriega in Panama." Holland put away his letter, raising an eyebrow at Boone. Boone just shrugged.

"Construction guys are working on some modifications to our urban combat range. Apparently there are some potential extractions that we'll be tasked for if we do actually go in, so we're gonna want to practice on several different building layouts. That's all we know for now. Until they get the range ready, all of you need to get your gear completely squared away for immediate deployment. That's all, fellas." He turned to leave.

"What about me, Lucky?" Holland spoke up. "I still haven't had my final board. I'm not gonna get left behind, am I?"

Flaherty looked back at him. "Oh, thanks for reminding me, Tulip. We're putting together a board for you this afternoon. Commander's conference room at fourteen hundred hours. That gives you about three hours to get ready." Flaherty headed out the door. "See you then."

Holland's mouth was hanging slightly open as he watched the officer leave.

"So," Boone said. "it's a good news, bad news, sorta thing. Good news, we finally get to go put all our training to use. Bad news, you have three hours to get ready for the hardest oral test you'll ever take, and if you fail that, you get to go back to the fleet and swab decks for a living - which would only be the most humiliating thing you could imagine. No pressure."

"You should look into becoming a motivational speaker, you know that?"

"Why?" Boone asked. "Did that motivate you?"

"Oh yeah. Motivated me to stuff a sock in your mouth."

Boone chuckled and stood up. "You'll do fine. C'mon. I'll give you a warm-up quiz."

Boone led the way to the rifle range, where he had Holland work at several quick reaction drills while Boone shouted random questions at him about everything from standard procedures and combat tactics to magazine capacities for every type of firearm he could think of, to proper gas mixtures for scuba tanks under various conditions. The oral exam Holland was facing that afternoon was his final hurdle in training before he could officially call himself a SEAL; he would have to sit in a room with several officers and senior enlisted SEALs, working out manual navigation problems or stripping weapons while they rapid-fired multiple questions at him, covering any topic they chose. The idea was to ensure that Holland's grasp of all the critical information he'd learned so far in his training wouldn't slip when he came under pressure.

He'd been preparing for the board since he passed BUD/S training almost four months earlier, but he'd had to fit that studying in around all of his other required training. Meeting and corresponding with Lexie had added another demand on his time and attention, and now he was concerned that he hadn't trained enough. By the time he and Boone came back from the range, he was feeling subdued.

"Why the long face, Meat?" Boone asked. "You did great, far as I could tell. It's gonna be a piece of cake."

"Was *your* board a piece of cake?"

"No. I wet myself right before I went in, I was so nervous. You might want to stop off at the head on your way."

Holland shook his head. "You are *so* bad at this."

"You're welcome," Boone said. "Look at it this way, brother.

There's no way that you'll ever know everything there is to know, about anything, all right? But at this point in your training, you have more information fresh in your mind than most of the old guys, because you've been eating, sleeping and breathing that stuff since you got here. So you just answer the questions you know with confidence. If they ask you something you don't know, you tell 'em with confidence that you don't know the answer, and you press the hell on, got it? Answer what you can and don't let the rest derail you."

Holland nodded. "All right. Thanks, I think." He looked at his watch. "I'd better get. Wish me luck."

"Luck's for suckers. The rest of us train."

"Right." Holland headed for the door.

"Good luck," Boone called after him. "Can I have your swim fins if you fail?"

Holland made a rude hand gesture, and went to face the board.

A week later, Holland barely remembered the nerves he'd felt prior to facing the board - he was too exhausted to think about it. He'd passed, and then he'd gone right back to training. The team had trained relentlessly on everything from helicopter insertions to beach infiltration to heavy weapons drills and combat first aid exercises.

They had just been forced to abort a helicopter assault on a mock-up of a three story building, because one of the team members had fallen from the helicopter when it was twenty feet above the roof. They were supposed to fast-rope to the roof from the aircraft by sliding down thick ropes and slowing their descent at the last minute by clenching their gloved hands around the rope. Holland's feet had just hit the roof when the SEAL on the opposite side of the aircraft had lost his grip on the rope and fell, striking the roof decking ten feet away with a sickening crunch.

The exercise had stopped instantly, and Holland and the other

SEALs had worked quickly to stabilize the man for evacuation to the hospital. Now, Lieutenant Flaherty, just back from the hospital, briefed the rest of the team.

"Woody's back is broken," Flaherty said. "Doc said it's too early to tell if he'll be able to walk again. They've got him sedated right now. You fellas take a break and go home. We'll start again at 0600 tomorrow."

The team slowly filed out of the building, each man heading to his own home. Every one of them was exhausted; every one realizing that it could have just as easily been them lying in the hospital with an uncertain future ahead of them.

The incident had badly rattled Holland. As he drove home, he knew he needed to talk with Lexie.

"One of the guys got hurt today," he said into the phone.

"Was it serious?" Lexie's voice sounded sympathetic and very far away.

"He fell out of a helicopter. Broke his back."

"I'm so sorry, Law."

"They're not sure if he'll ever walk again, and even if he does, his career is probably finished."

There was an uncomfortable silence before she asked, "Are *you* okay?"

"I'm good, Lexie. I'm worried about you, to be honest."

"You shouldn't be."

"I think I should. Listen, I really need to get something off my chest." Lexie didn't respond, just waited for him to vent. "I'm not being fair to you, Lex."

"Law, you're not going to go there *again*, are you?"

"It's the truth. It's not fair to expect you to have a relationship with a guy who might have to leave you at the drop of a hat, and maybe never come back - or come back crippled, like Woody. I feel like I'm dragging you into something that you'll regret later."

"I haven't complained so far."

"I know that. But I just don't want to put you into a position where you have a reason to."

"Lawson. What are you saying?"

He took a deep breath. "I think I need to let you go, Lexie."

Her silence stretched into several long moments.

"Lexie? You still there?"

"I'm here," she said in a soft voice.

"Lex, believe me, I'm really sorry about this. I just don't want you to be one of those wives who loses her husband and never gets to know why he died, or even if his death was worth it. I don't want to be responsible for leaving you alone in the world."

"So, to avoid leaving me alone, you're going to leave me alone?" Finally, there was a hint of anger in her voice. "That has to be the most ridiculous reasoning I've ever heard for anything."

"That's not what I meant," Holland said. "I just don't want to cause you pain."

"So you're going to run away? As I just said, that makes no sense. This is just a shock to me, Law. I never imagined that you'd be taking the coward's way out."

"I'm not a coward." His protest sounded pathetic, even to his own ears. "I'm trying to protect you."

She scoffed. "You don't hurt people and pretend it's a help, Law." She took a deep breath. "Look. I'm not really sure what it is that you want, but let me make it easy for you. I never complained about what you do for a living, and I've never asked you to leave. If you still think that's what you need to do, I can't stop you - that has to be your choice. But I'm not going to try to change your mind."

Holland was silent. He felt like his entire world was crumbling, and he was helpless to stop it. He wanted to say something to fix this whole mess that he'd created, but when the words wouldn't come, Lexie spoke for him.

"Good-bye, Lawson."

CHAPTER FOUR

Execution

Howard Air Force Base
   Panama City, Panama
   December 20, 1989
   0030 Local Time

"Saddle up, boys!" Lieutenant Flaherty came into the hangar, weighed down by a massive amount of gear and weapons. "You all know your jobs, so let's go to work!"

The SEALs rose to their feet, collected their gear and started loading into five UH60 Blackhawk helicopters. Each helicopter also carried a collapsed Combat Rubber Raiding Craft, or CRRC, slung under the fuselage between the landing gear. The CRRCs were fifteen feet long when fully inflated and each could transport ten SEALs plus their gear. The plan called for the SEALs to be dropped two miles off shore, where they would inflate their CRRCs and continue to shore, assaulting the airfield from the sea.

Boone and Holland were at the back of the hangar, loading

into an MH6 Little Bird chopper with four other men. They had a different mission. The rest of the team was slated to hit Paitilla Airfield with the objective of destroying Manuel Noriega's personal jet, eliminating it as a possible means for the dictator to flee the country. The SEALs would drop from the Blackhawks into the water of Panama Bay, then take the CRRCs to the beach adjacent to the airfield. From there, they would secure the field and disable Noriega's jet if he attempted to use it.

Meanwhile, Boone's team was going to hit a prison in Panama City known as the Cárcel Modelo, where an American citizen was being held by Noriega's forces. The American had been arrested several weeks earlier and charged with espionage, and the State Department was convinced he would be murdered as soon as the invasion kicked off. The SEALs were tasked to hit the jail fifteen minutes before H-hour for the main assault, which would go off at 0100 hours, in order to maintain the element of surprise. Launching the two separate assault elements close to the same time would allow the airport assault team time to get into position while the jail team hit their target.

The overhead hangar lights went out, and the hangar doors slowly started to open. Flaherty came over and slapped Holland on the shoulder. "Ready, girls?"

Holland just nodded as he hefted his Harris-McMillan M86 sniper rifle. Boone answered for him. "We're good to go, Lucky. Y'all be careful."

Flaherty smiled, his teeth showing bright in contrast to the dark camouflage paint on his face. "The intel guys are still saying we should expect light resistance, but we all know what military intelligence is good for. Still, we'll be good."

"I dunno, boss. You got so many guys hitting that airport, seems like it'd be a better idea to just let the Army handle it. If overwhelming numbers is your tool of choice, the Army's the best option - not the SEALs."

"Yeah, well," Flaherty looked back at the Blackhawks, loaded with three platoons of SEALs plus support personnel - almost fifty men. "I guess the Army didn't get the memo." He looked back at Boone. "'Ours is not to reason why.'"

Boone nodded. "'Into the valley of Death, rode the Squid Half-Hundred.'"

Flaherty laughed at Boone's butchered paraphrase of the Tennyson poem. "You are *such* a knucklehead, Ballroom."

"Laughter's the best medicine, boss. Hey, if you guys catch Noriega trying to get on his plane, slap him around some for me, will ya?"

Flaherty laughed again. "I'll do that. Honestly, you fellas have the harder job tonight. That prison isn't likely to be 'lightly' defended. You watch your backs."

"You got it." Boone took Flaherty's hand. Flaherty reached up and gave him a playful smack on the side of the head, then went around to the rest of the team and shook each man's hand in turn before heading back to his own helicopter.

The group of Blackhawks were already firing up their engines as the last men climbed aboard. Outside, the airfield was blacked out. As the first of the helicopters started taxiing outside, Boone took up a position in the side door of the Little Bird next to Holland. They sat with their legs hanging out the door, feet braced on the landing skid.

"How's yer head, brother?" Boone shouted over the growing whine of the engines.

"It's still screwed on," Holland shouted back. "Mostly straight, too. This is what we came here for, right?"

"Too right." Boone looked at his friend for a moment, then draped an arm across the younger man's shoulder. "We'll be drinking Mai Tais on the beach twelve hours from now."

"What's a Mai Tai?" Holland shouted.

Boone laughed as the helicopter slowly rose a few feet off the hangar floor and drifted toward the open doors. "You've led a sheltered life, my boy, but don't worry about it. Uncle Boone will educate you proper-like."

"That's just what I need," Holland said, staring out at the

black night as the chopper cleared the doorway and started to climb. "More wisdom from the ballroom dance warrior."

They both laughed as the night swallowed their blacked-out aircraft. They were going to war.

TALON 26
Over Panama Bay
Five Miles South of Panama City
0040 Local Time

"Say again?" Flaherty shouted into his headset.

The helicopter pilot shouted back. "Command says they moved H-hour up by fifteen minutes. They claim you guys were supposed to be in the water ten minutes ago."

"You gotta be kidding me!" Flaherty was livid. "Ten minutes ago, they said we were on schedule, and we hadn't even left the hangar! What do they think this thing is, a time machine?"

"Sorry, lieutenant," the pilot said. "I'm just the messenger here. That's all they told me."

Flaherty was standing in the cargo bay, just aft of the cockpit. He stared out the windscreen, frantically doing mental calculations. "All right, here's the deal then. I'm gonna need you to drop us closer in to shore."

"How close? We get any closer than this, and the PDF guys at the airport are gonna hear us for sure. That's what you brought those fancy rubber boats for, isn't it?"

"We don't have a choice. There's a spot right off the south end of the runway, three hundred yards out, where the water's deep enough for us to drop from about ten feet up. Can you get us in that close, and just make a quick pass perpendicular to the runway center line? We'll bail out with the boats and work our way to shore from there."

"You aren't worried the PDF will think five helicopters milling around right offshore is suspicious?"

"You're not gonna be milling around. All five helos will make a pass west to east in a single line, fifty meters between each aircraft. We all go out the door simultaneously when the lead ship gets to my mark - I'll have you flare for just a moment to give us time to get clear. Can you do that?"

"No problem."

The pilot started relaying the change of plans to the other aircraft in the flight, and Flaherty did the same over the SEAL radio net. By the time everyone in all five helicopters knew what they were doing, Flaherty's pilot was shouting back at him.

"Airfield's coming up fast, eleven o'clock!"

Flaherty leaned in between the pilot and copilot, pointing through the windscreen. "See where they've built the seawall up slightly higher just past the southeast corner of the runway?"

"Yeah, I got it."

"Okay, you're gonna want to put that part of the wall directly off your left side, and you want to be lined up three hundred yards off shore. Get us down low and flare right there with the others behind you as close as they can get, and we'll take care of the rest."

"No problem. Twenty seconds."

"Twenty seconds," Flaherty repeated over the SEALs' frequency.

HAWK 77
Over Panama Bay
Five Miles Southwest of Panama City

"Unbelievable!" Boone fumed, taking his hand away from his headset. "Those rear echelon idiots are claiming we're already ten minutes behind schedule!"

"How do they figure?" Holland shouted into his mic over the noise of the Little Bird.

"They figure, because the Army changed the damn timetable

at the last minute, and didn't bother to tell us Navy guys about it!"

"What are we gonna do?"

"We're gonna go faster." Boone switched to the intercom so the pilots could hear him. "Fellas, since command thinks we're behind, we're gonna have to beat feet. Everybody else in country is gonna start shooting in a couple of minutes, which means we're about to lose the element of surprise."

"Roger that," the pilot responded. "We're inbound now."

The aircraft pitched into a nose-down attitude as the pilot increased power and raced toward the city. Looking ahead, Holland could already see random specks of light flickering among the buildings. Muzzle flashes. He smacked Boone on the shoulder and pointed. "Looks like they're starting without us."

Boone swore again, then keyed his mic and addressed the whole team. "All right, guys, we're going in hot. Assume the guards at the Cárcel Modelo are alerted. Even if we do manage to get there before they kill our guy, there's definitely gonna be a shootout."

TALON 26
Approaching Paitilla Airfield
0042 Local Time

The Blackhawks swept in low and fast over the water, at the last second pitching their noses up in perfect synchronization in order to bleed off speed. Flaherty, now standing in the center of the cargo bay and closely watching their approach, didn't wait for word from the pilot. As soon as their forward motion was checked, he keyed his microphone again.

"GO GO GO!"

Fifty men hit the water at the same time, along with all five CRRCs. The helicopters added power and raced away, frothing the surface of the bay with spindrift from their rotor wash. As soon as the SEALs resurfaced, five of them worked quickly to attach scuba tanks to the nozzles on each CRRC, rapidly inflating the rafts. Other men mounted the small outboard engines that had been slung inside the CRRCs. The empty scuba tanks were quickly disconnected and dropped overboard, the engines came to life, and the men piled into the rafts. Each boat had five men inside and five more clinging prone to the pylons along each side. The raft leaders each reported ready on the team radio net, and they all sped off together toward the sea wall at the edge of the airfield. Less than two minutes had passed since they'd hit the water.

HAWK 77
Over Panama City

When Holland had graduated first in his class from his combat sniper course several months earlier, he hadn't imagined needing to put his skills to the test quite so soon, but as they closed on the target building, he barely thought about it. Now, as they passed over the crowded neighborhood around the Cárcel Modelo prison, small arms fire peppered the Little Bird. Strapped to the deck of the chopper at the end of a safety tether, Holland leaned forward against the stock of his rifle and scanned for the sources of the ground fire.

A soldier appeared on the roof of La Commandancia, the PDF Headquarters building that stood across the street from the prison to the north. As the man raised a rocket propelled grenade launcher and swung it toward the chopper, Holland squeezed off the first combat round of his career.

The .300 Winchester Magnum slug took the soldier in the chest, knocking him backward. As he fell, he pulled the trigger on his launcher, sending the RPG pirouetting skyward like a clumsy bottle rocket. Next to Holland, Boone was firing controlled bursts from his Squad Automatic Weapon. Out of the corner of his eye, Holland could see some PDF armored personnel carriers several blocks away, moving in their direction. He shot a man running along the north wall of the Cárcel Modelo, and the man crumpled in a heap. Two men exited a rooftop doorway, and he quickly cycled the bolt on the M86 and shot the first, who collapsed and slid several feet across the flat roof on his face.

"Don't you ever miss?" Boone hollered next to him.

Holland ignored him, cycling the bolt again and taking a bead on the second man, who was just diving back through the doorway. Holland fired just as the man pulled the door closed behind him, and the bullet smashed into the door a fraction of a second too late.

"Apparently, I do, on occasion."

"Happens to the best of us," Boone chuckled as he loosed another burst at two men on the south parapet. "Roof's clear!" he shouted to the pilot. The Little Bird immediately slewed sideways toward the main roof of the prison. As soon as it crossed the parapet, the pilot checked its motion and the SEALs piled out. Holland almost forgot to disconnect his safety harness from his belt. The two or three seconds it took to fumble with the release put him at the back of the group moving to the rooftop door as the helicopter dusted off and moved away, to wait a short distance away for the SEALs to finish their building assault.

Boone was first through the door as another SEAL yanked it open. The rest of the team flowed through the door right on his heels, but Boone almost tripped over a dead man at the top of the stairs. It was the man they'd thought Holland had narrowly missed. Holland's bullet had passed through the door and struck the guard in the back of the head as he tried to escape.

"Clear!" Boone shouted. He glanced down at the dead man. "Looks like you didn't miss after all, Tulip."

"Sure I did," Holland said. "That shot was a foot and a half high - I was aiming for center mass."

Boone shook his head. "Showoff." The team continued downstairs toward the cell block where the American was reportedly being held. "I'm gonna have to quit calling you 'Tulip'," Boone said as they came to a locked steel door on the second floor. Another SEAL took a knee and quickly set a plastic explosive charge against the lock.

"Great," Holland said, flattening himself against the wall a couple of feet right of the doorway. "What are you gonna call me now?"

"Hit it," Boone told the other SEAL, who pressed the detonator. The explosion bent the door inward like a taco shell. This time Holland was first through the door, shoving it out of the way and rushing into a hall on the other side. He shot a dazed guard who was staggering down the hall toward them, carrying an AK-47 in his hands. Another guard stepped out of a crossing hall, and Holland smoothly dropped his now empty rifle, letting it dangle by the sling around his chest. In the same motion, he pulled his service pistol and shot the second guard twice before the man could bring his own weapon to bear.

"Clear!" Holland shouted.

"'Long Arm Lawson'," Boone said, striding past Holland with his SAW shouldered and ready. "Long Arm of the Law, son. Get it?"

Holland grinned in spite of himself. He holstered his pistol, slapped a fresh magazine into his rifle and chambered a round, then drew his pistol again and fell into line behind the rest of the men.

CHAPTER FIVE

Goat Rope

Paitilla Airfield
Panama City
0053 Local Time

Flaherty and the rest of the SEALS were lying prone on the rocks of the sea wall at the south end of the runway, scanning the airfield for PDF troops. Other SEAL teams had done preliminary reconnaissance on the field over the past several months, but through some warped bit of thinking at a much higher pay grade than Flaherty's, it had been determined that the assault would be carried out completely by troops from 'off-site'.

This meant that almost sixty percent of Flaherty's force had been in-country for less than a week. Their familiarity with their objective was limited to what the outgoing teams had been able to provide in hurried briefings before they got on a plane and left for home. This all made Flaherty more than a little bit annoyed, as well as slightly nervous. There was nothing, he knew, quite like first-hand experience. Sometimes, it might be the only difference between success and disaster.

Based on the intelligence he'd received from the recon teams, Flaherty knew there was a sizable hole already cut in the airport perimeter fence, and it hadn't been repaired as of two days ago. He could use that hole as a point of entry for his entire force, saving time, but it would also concentrate them all in one place, making them easy targets for any hidden ambushers. He decided to go with a slightly modified plan.

Flaherty tasked four men to take two of the CRRCs around the east side of the airfield, about halfway up the length of the runway. Noriega's plane was housed in a cluster of hangars at the north end of the airport. From this far south, Flaherty couldn't make out details of those buildings well enough to determine PDF troop strength on the field, if any. At the moment, it all looked quiet, but looks can be deceiving. Flaherty would use the two pairs of SEALs to hook around the east side of the field and get closer to the runway midpoint and the buildings at the north end, where they could act as spotters for the larger force from the south. There was virtually no cover on the south and east sides of the field, and Flaherty didn't want to expose his force without first determining what they were facing.

As the two CRRCs departed, the rest of Flaherty's force crept closer to the fence, cutting three new holes at intervals while staying as low as possible. Once inside the fence, they would be at least marginally safe up to the runway edge, concealed by the gentle slope of dirt and rock leading down to the water; but they would still have to cover the distance to the hangars eventually. He wanted to be sure that he wasn't leading his men into a trap.

Cárcel Modelo Prison

Moving through the cell block, the team quickly located the American hostage. Shouting through the locked door, Boone directed the man to pull his mattress over him and get down on the floor, then they set a charge on the lock. When it detonated, three SEALs rushed into the tiny cell. Boone yanked the mattress off of the cowering man while another SEAL aimed a powerful flashlight at the man's face.

"WHAT'S YOUR NAME?" Boone shouted.

"Mills!" the terrified man answered. "Kent Mills!"

Boone reached down and lifted the man's chin. "Jackpot! Get that armor in here!"

Another SEAL produced a ballistic vest and helmet, which Boone and the others helped Mills into. Once he was set, they headed back toward the roof, and Boone got on the radio.

"HAWK, this is FOX; Jackpot - I say again, Jackpot. Exfil in thirty seconds."

"Roger that, FOX. HAWK is inbound."

"Our ride's on the way, fellas," Boone said. "Let's make ourselves scarce." They all picked up their pace, running up the stairs to the roof with Mills almost being carried between them. He was wide-eyed and looked to be on the verge of panic, but for the moment he was holding it together well enough.

At the top of the stairs, Holland took a knee just inside the door and scanned the roof and surrounding buildings outside. He could hear the helicopter approaching, but couldn't yet see it. A man opened a window on the fifth floor of a building across the street to the west and aimed a rifle in the direction of the Little Bird. Holland fired a single shot, and the man fell backward into the room, out of sight.

"Hostiles in the west building," he reported. More gunfire was erupting outside now as the helicopter slid into view, crossing the parapet from the south. "Move up." Two of the SEALs slid past Holland and emerged onto the roof, taking up positions either side of the doorway. Almost immediately, they were both firing to the north and west.

"Moving!" Holland stepped through the door and took a knee on the roof just beyond. He shot at another man in a different window across the street to the west, then shifted his attention to the roof of La Commandancia, where more troops were gathering. Boone and the remaining two SEALs waited inside the stairwell with Mills. Holland fired twice more as the helicopter came to a hover inches above the roof decking. "GO GO GO!" He reloaded as Boone and the others brought Mills out and ran for the chopper.

The rate of enemy gunfire was rapidly increasing now. Holland could hear rounds impacting the chopper as he waved the two SEALs kneeling beside him to board the aircraft. He took two more shots as they ran, then got up and followed them aboard. Boone hollered at the pilot, and they were airborne. Holland and the others continued firing at the troops on the roof of La Commandancia as they lifted off. He was just beginning to think they were away clean when a loud bang came from the rear of the helicopter.

Multiple alarms immediately went off, and the engine started racing wildly. The aircraft lurched into a sickening spin as the pilot struggled to control it, but something had destroyed the tail rotor. They were going down - the only question was whether or not they'd survive the crash.

Paitilla Airfield
0106 Local Time

"All quiet." The report from the second of Flaherty's scout teams echoed the first - there was no visible movement on the airfield. The east side of the field was unlit, but the hangars on the west side had several bright floodlights on their roofs pointing to the east, illuminating everything brightly. The insides of the hangars were unlit, and the bright floodlights above the open doors made it all but impossible to see inside clearly.

Still, the scouts had said it was all clear.

"All right," Flaherty answered. "Main element's crossing the wire."

"We oughta have the scouts take out those lights, Lucky." Master Chief Don Jardine whispered. "Anybody coming up the runway or across it from the east is gonna be in full view of those hangars."

Flaherty paused. "Scouts said it was clear."

"They said it was *quiet*, L-T. That ain't the same thing."

Flaherty outranked Jardine and was technically in command, but he would have been foolish to ignore the more experienced man's advice. He took a breath, and was about to contact the scouts again when a transmission from the helicopter they'd come in on interrupted him.

"Green Six, Talon Two-Six."

"Go, Talon Two-Six," Flaherty answered.

"Green Six, be advised, intel reports PDF armor inbound your location. ETA five minutes."

"Talon Two-Six, say numbers."

"Report said three to five V-300 APCs. No intel on armament. Sorry for the delay, I'm just relaying messages to you through a third party; no direct link to command. It takes a while. Standby."

The V-300 was a lightly armored American-made troop transport capable of transporting nine soldiers and carrying anything from 7.62 millimeter machine guns to a 90 millimeter cannon. Flaherty knew he was potentially facing up to forty-five enemy soldiers, maybe more, supported by much heavier weapons than his team had. He waited for the pilot of TALON 26 to continue, but when the radio silence dragged, he keyed his mic.

"Talon Two-Six, Green Six."

No response.

Flaherty ground his teeth. "Talon Two-Six, Green Six."

"Green Six, Talon Two-Six."

"You have anything else for me, Two-Six?"

"Affirmative, Green Six. Command directs you to assault your primary objective immediately. Inbound armor could be transport for principal player; proceed with all possible speed. Command also directs

you to inflict minimal damage on your target."

Flaherty was stunned. "'Minimal damage'?" he replied. "What the hell does that mean, Two-Six? They want us to take it out with stern language?"

"Sorry, Green Six," the pilot said. *"That's the order they passed to us. They didn't elaborate - just said 'minimal damage.'"*

"Roger, Two-Six," Flaherty answered, disgusted. "Green Six out." He switched to the team frequency. "Green One, Green Two; We've got possibly five PDF APCs inbound, command thinks they're bringing Noriega to the airport. Take out those lights - we're moving to your position."

Flaherty had wanted to leapfrog his men up the runway in twos, separated by wide intervals to keep them from presenting too much of a target. But with enemy armor inbound, he knew they had no time left for that. They had to get to Noriega's plane before the dictator's troops arrived in force. The last thing Flaherty wanted was to slug it out with a larger force. If he could take out the jet before the troops arrived with Noriega, they'd be likely to take their commander elsewhere, removing the need for a fight.

Master Chief Jardine was already waving his men into position. Shots started to ring out from the north as the scouts opened fire on the floodlights, and the airfield was plunged into semi-darkness. Flaherty slithered through one of the holes in the perimeter fence and climbed the low embankment to the edge of the runway, glancing back at his men.

"Let's go *gently* break a plane, boys!"

HAWK 77
Over Panama City

The Little Bird lurched as the tail empennage smacked the corner of a tall building. Holland, last to board the chopper, had failed to clip on to the safety strap, and now the centrifugal force of the spinning aircraft was rapidly becoming more than he could resist. He slid toward the side door, desperately grabbing for a handhold as he went.

He had a brief view of the street far below him, and he was certain he was going to die, but the trajectory of the chopper brought him over the roof of a shorter building just as he slid out the open door. He only fell about eight feet before smacking down on the flat roof, knocking the wind out of him. He heard the chopper hit the street seconds later, amid breaking glass, tearing sheet metal and the constant staccato of automatic weapons fire.

Rolling into a crouch, Holland forced himself to the low parapet and peeked over. The Little Bird was on its right side in an intersection, half of the nose jammed through the smashed windows of a store front. There was a great deal of smoke and dust, but no fire. Men were crawling from the wreckage. He moved to the corner of the roof where he could see up and down the roads in all four directions away from the intersection. A crowd was forming several blocks to the west, but most of the gunfire was coming from the direction of the Cárcel Modelo, which he guessed was several blocks to the northeast.

Looking to the north, he saw several PDF soldiers running across the street two blocks away from the crash site. One of them was carrying an RPG, and took a knee in the middle of the street, facing the crash. Holland shot him before he could fire.

"Long Arm, is that you up there?" Boone's voice sounded surprised in his earpiece.

"Hey, Ballroom," Holland replied, watching the now-empty street to the north. "I'm good to go, but I might need you to call a fire truck to get me down from here. What's your status?"

"All accounted for, now. Everybody's alive, but we're all banged up pretty good."

"Okay," Holland said as he scanned the street. "I can be your overwatch, at least for a while. You've got hostiles mixed in with civilians to the west, and more hostiles to the north and east. The south road looks clear for the moment."

"Copy all, Long Arm. We'll move out as soon as you get down here."

Boone had barely finished speaking when an RPG whistled across the intersection from the west and detonated against the side of the store where the Little Bird was lodged. Glass and shrapnel showered the street below.

Holland swung his rifle to the west, and saw the crowd had grown larger. Two men in red shirts were at the front of the press, waving weapons overhead and haranguing the crowd, urging them to advance on the crash. The red shirts were a common sign of membership in one of Noriega's so-called Dignity Battalions, which were mostly a collection of off-duty PDF troops and civilian thugs who terrorized the civilian population at Noriega's direction. Nicknamed 'Dingbats' by American forces in the country, they were an untrained, undisciplined and mostly uncontrolled militia. As individuals they were not much of a threat, but at the head of a mob, they could become dangerous. These two men were clearly trying to get the mob to charge the helicopter. Abruptly, they both turned and headed toward Boone's group, and the crowd followed in ragged order.

Holland shot the closest man first, then quickly cycled the bolt and shot the other as well. Both men collapsed on the pavement and went still. The crowd, visibly flinching at the shots as if it were one huge organism, hesitated.

"Ballroom, you gotta go!" Holland barked into his headset. "You've got a mob inbound from the west. Move out, I'll cover!"

"Roger," Boone answered. *"We're bugging out to the south. Meet us at the beach, I'll try to call for evac on the way."*

Holland fired another shot, this time hitting a truck loaded with men approaching from the east. The windshield spider-webbed as his bullet passed through, and the driver quickly reconsidered his route and wrenched the truck down a side street and out of the line of fire. Holland reloaded, then peeked over the parapet again and saw that Boone's group was shuffling off to the south, so he got up and ran along ahead of them, jumping from roof to roof along the row of attached buildings.

Paitilla Airfield
0108 Local Time

Flaherty's group was almost to the north end of the airport when the lights suddenly came back on. All the runway edge lighting, which had been off before, as well as more floodlights around the hangars, switched on at once. Caught in the open, the SEALs could do nothing but continue. Flaherty shouted at his scout teams to kill the new lights. They started shooting again; but the enemy suddenly opened up as well.

Several Panamanians had been well hidden inside the hangars, invisible behind barrels and crates. They had waited as the Americans moved up the field, patiently holding their position as the scouts took out the first bank of flood lights. Now as the second bank lit up the field, they had a clear view of nearly fifty men spread out across the runway less than a hundred yards from their position, totally exposed.

The Panamanians were armed with two AK-47 assault rifles and one PKM machine gun mounted on a low tripod. Firing down the open runway at exposed targets, those three weapons proved more than enough. Some of their shots were low, but the bullets ricocheted off the tarmac and still found their marks; but for the most part, their aim was murderously accurate.

Half a mile from the airport, as the SEALs suffered in the open under withering fire, a group of five Panamanian APCs sped past the airport access road without even slowing down.

They hadn't been going to Paitilla after all, and the SEALs had been ordered into a frontal assault for no reason.

El Chorrillo Neighborhood
Panama City

Boone's group only made it three blocks before they were cut off by another crowd. Holland directed them down a cross street to the east, but found he could no longer follow, as his way was now blocked by taller buildings and wider alleys that he couldn't jump across. He had to get down off the roof.

While they were running, Boone had managed to contact an AC-130 Spectre gunship that was orbiting over La Commandancia, firing 40 millimeter rounds into the PDF headquarters in preparation for an incoming Army assault on the complex. The Spectre pilot had relayed Boone's position to command, and the Army was now sending several APCs to come and pick the team up, but their ETA was anybody's guess. For the time being, they had to keep moving.

"Ballroom, I'm blocked up here, I need to get down." Holland radioed as Boone directed his group around an open plaza.

"Roger that. We'll set up a perimeter and wait for you."

"Negative," Holland said. *"That crowd is almost to the intersection behind you. Break to the south and I'll catch up."*

Boone didn't like it, but he knew he had no choice. Every man on his team was injured from the crash or from minor bullet wounds, and the crowds were closing in. They had to get Mills to safety as soon as possible, and if they waited for Holland, they all might be killed. Boone whistled at the SEAL that was on point, and waved him to the south.

"Roger, Long Arm. Don't be too far behind. We should have a ride coming soon."

"I'll be along shortly," Holland said. Then he ran to the back of the building and looked for a way down into the alley.

Paitilla Airfield

Flaherty was at the front of the line of advancing SEALs when the Panamanian defenders opened fire. One round smashed his right knee at the same time as another hit him square in the throat, just above the top edge of his body armor. He collapsed in the middle of the runway. Master Chief Jardine dropped to a knee in front of him, quickly assessing his wounds while using his own body as a shield to protect his commander.

Jardine barked orders at the other SEALs, directing them toward the source of the incoming fire. Looking around, he saw at least ten men were already down, sprawled on the pavement. A couple of them were still returning fire in spite of their injuries, but several weren't moving at all.

A bullet smashed into Jardine's left shoulder, knocking him backward over Flaherty's prone form. He struggled upright and fired two short bursts into the second open hangar to his left, where he could see muzzle flashes illuminating the nose of a parked Learjet.

'Minimal damage', my eye, Jardine thought. He looked around. "Lance!" he bellowed. "AT-4, middle hangar!"

To Jardine's right, Lance Pennell, one of the SEALs who had welcomed Holland when he first arrived at Little Creek months before, unslung an AT-4 rocket launcher from his back and fired it through the open hangar door where Noriega's jet was parked. The rocket pierced the right side of the aircraft just aft of the cockpit, destroying electronics and controls and starting a small fire.

That plane won't be going anywhere, Jardine thought, as he grabbed Flaherty by the back of his body armor and started dragging him away from the fight. Out of the corner of his eye, he saw Lance suddenly go down, shot in the head. Jardine was shouting for a medic when something slammed into his spine, and everything went black.

CHAPTER SIX

Collateral

El Chorrillo Neighborhood

Holland dropped into the alley, having climbed down from the roof by lowering himself down a drain pipe and several dangling clotheslines. Quickly, he moved to the shadows near the alley entrance and scanned the street beyond. Smoke wafted down the street in dirty ribbons, fed by various fires throughout the area. People were running back and forth in random directions, while at the street corner to his north, several Dignity Battalion members were enthusiastically smashing store windows.

Holland keyed his radio and spoke softly into the mic. "Ballroom, Long Arm - how do you hear?"

Static.

"Ballroom, Long Arm, radio check." Holland waited several more seconds with no answer. He was about to key up again when a barrage of gunfire erupted nearby, followed by several people running past the alley in panic. He raised his rifle and edged closer to the street.

A young woman passed in front of the alley, but halfway across, she was suddenly grabbed by the hair from behind by a man wearing a dirty red Dignity Battalion t-shirt. The woman screamed and struggled, but the man slapped her and dragged her into the alley, followed closely by another Dingbat. The first man was swearing at the woman in Spanish, and the second man was stealing nervous glances behind them while hurrying to catch up to his friend.

They shoved the woman against the wall on the left side of the alley. The first man slapped her again, knocking her to the ground. He said something to his buddy, who laughed. Then the first man pulled a knife from his belt and squatted down on his heels, showing the blade to the woman and leering at her.

The report of Holland's Sig-Sauer P226 pistol seemed almost deafening in the narrow alley. The man with the knife wavered drunkenly on his heels, then simply fell over, a black hole in his left temple oozing blood. Most of the right side of his head was spattered on his friend's jeans and shirt, but Holland put two rounds in the second man's chest before he had time to recover from the shock of seeing his friend killed at close range. The woman screamed louder, staring in horror at the painted-faced apparition that appeared out of the shadows and stood over her.

Holland quickly checked the two bodies for vital signs and other weapons, then trotted to the mouth of the alley and looked up and down the street. The woman was alternating between sobs and shrieks when he came back to her.

"Quiet down," he said, holding a single finger to his lips. She looked at him like she expected him to grow horns, and kept screaming.

"Silencio!" he barked at her, expending his entire repertoire of Spanish language skills in one word. Her shrieks went down a couple of decibels, but she was still wide-eyed and panic-stricken. He held his finger to his lips again, and went back to look down the street.

"Do you speak English?" he asked when he came back to her.

She was breathing rapidly now, but had managed to stop screaming. She nodded her head. "Yes, I speak English." She looked sideways at the two dead men on the ground next to her, and looked like she would start screaming all over again.

Holland holstered his pistol and gently helped her to her feet. "You live around here?"

She nodded. "Bodega," she said, pointing to the north. "Mi familia -" she broke into another round of sobs.

Holland went back to the end of the alley and looked up the street to the north. The storefront he'd seen the Dingbats smashing out moments before was now almost completely obscured by smoke. The crowd had dispersed, but the bodega the woman spoke of was going to be a total loss. Holland could see flames showing through the smoke already.

"Was your family at home?" he asked.

She nodded, remembering to use English. "My mother, my father..." She looked down at the two bodies. "They killed them."

Holland looked at her again, realizing she was much younger than he'd first thought. Maybe eighteen or nineteen, she'd just witnessed her parents being murdered, then seen the murderers killed right in front of her. "Do you have someplace else you can go? Other family members?"

She just shook her head, tears starting to flow again.

Holland thought about his options. He couldn't leave this girl behind in the middle of an urban battlefield, especially if she had no safe place to go. With gangs of Dingbats roaming the streets, a pretty young girl like her was far from safe out in the open. He was in grave danger himself if he remained in this neighborhood, but taking her with him could slow him down or attract even more unwanted attention. He needed to link up with the rest of Boone's team before the Army APCs showed up and spirited them all away, or he'd be left behind.

"Come on," he said, making up his mind and taking her carefully by the arm. "We need to move."

"But, my parents…"

"Are beyond our help," he said sharply, lowering his head and looking directly in her eyes. "If we want to survive the night, we have to get out of here, right now. You cannot go back home - it's gone. You understand? You can't go back there. Come with me, and I'll see to it that you're safe until things calm down, all right?"

She stared at him wide-eyed for a heartbeat, then nodded. Holland led her to the end of the alley and looked out one more time, then pulled her along in his wake as he headed south. She glanced back over her shoulder, grieving at the sight of her home in flames.

Boone looked around the corner of an apartment building, only to find more chaos. It seemed the entire city was awake, and people were either running aimlessly in panic, or they were rioting and looting. Getting their group of five SEALs, two pilots and one hostage through the constantly shifting and moving crowds was proving almost impossible. The only person in his group that was uninjured was Mills, the civilian, and to his credit, he'd asked for a firearm so he could help defend the group. Boone, unable to stop picturing a bloody last stand scenario, had given him a pistol.

They were less than a mile from the water now. The buildings had changed from multiple story tenements to more upscale apartments mixed with higher end shops. The looting here was worse than it had been closer to the prison, and they'd already had to fight their way through one group of particularly determined thieves when they could find no way around them.

The helicopter pilot was in bad shape with a concussion and a back injury, and Boone's own back ached every time he took a step. The rest of the group was in similar shape. They needed help, fast.

Boone held up a cautionary hand, warning his men to stay back as he watched the street. Some teenagers were busily lighting trash on fire in barrels, then rolling the barrels down the street toward Panama Bay, whooping and hollering louder each time. There was a large Catholic church five blocks away, but there was no way they could reach it without being seen.

Looking up and down the street, Boone knew they were running out of time. They had to get away, but the crowds were becoming so widespread that they could no longer move in the open without being spotted by someone. Boone drew away from the corner, then motioned one of his men to check the front door on the apartment building. It was locked, with a steel mesh door set in a heavy steel frame.

"Breach," Boone said. Another SEAL produced a block of plastic explosive and quickly set charges on the lock and both hinges. They all pressed themselves against the wall, and the man hit the detonator, smashing the security door into a tangle of metal. Two men went to work yanking it clear of the inner door while Boone tried the radio again.

"Long Arm, Ballroom - how do you hear?" There was no response. Boone was getting more concerned about Holland by the minute. "Long Arm, this is Ballroom. If you can hear me, we're about a mile from the beach. It's gettin' crowded down here, so you need to catch up. There's a big church between us and the beach, but we're held up a few blocks short of it -"

A truck suddenly careened around the corner and bore down on them. Men were jammed tightly into the bed, several of them sitting on the rails with one leg dangling over the side. They were mostly armed with sticks and clubs, but two men on the passenger side had AK-47s, which they raised as soon as they spotted the group of Americans. One man got off a wild burst that stitched a line across the second floor windows over Boone's head. The other man's rifle jammed.

The SEALs responded as one, each of them firing controlled bursts at different spots on the truck. Tires blew out, glass shattered, the hood flew open as a cloud of steam billowed from the radiator, and the truck veered off, jumping the curb and plowing into the side of a building half a block away. Up the street to the north, a crowd materialized out of the ragged skeins of smoke hanging over the neighborhood and moved toward them.

Boone turned to the men on the door, who had just smashed the inner door open and were starting to head inside. "Forget it!" he shouted, pointing up the street at the approaching crowd. "I don't want to get bottled up in there. Carl, Monty - you two take point; head for the church. Dane and Marvin, you guys are rear guard. You three," he nodded at Mills and the two pilots, "are with me in the middle. Everybody stay in sight of each other, and move fast. Let's go!"

Carl and Monty nodded, then took off toward the church at a trot, weapons up and scanning for threats. Boone let them get ten yards ahead. "Our turn, boys. Stay close." He took off after the first two men with his three charges close on his heels. Dane and Marvin let the group get ten yards away, then followed in their wake, checking behind them carefully for any signs of pursuit, but in the darkness and smoke-filled confusion, their group melted from view like shadows.

"What's your name?" Holland offered the girl his canteen. They had broken into an abandoned storefront to get off the street and catch their breath.

"Magdalena." She kept a wary eye on him while she took a small sip. She seemed almost willing to accept that he wasn't an immediate threat.

"I'm Lawson."

"Why are you here?" She ignored his introduction and handed the canteen back.

"Seriously?"

She blinked at him, and cocked her head slightly.

"Okay. I'm here because Noriega declared war on my country, among other reasons."

"What reasons?"

"Declaring war on us isn't enough?"

"If a bully only says he's fighting you, do you have to prove him right?"

Holland smiled at that. "I guess not. But he's broken the treaty between my country and yours multiple times, and he's been harassing Americans in the Canal Zone for months. The PDF killed a Marine a couple of days ago at an illegal roadblock; then they kidnapped another officer and his wife. Tortured the officer and terrorized his wife all night. Should we just sit back and twiddle our thumbs?"

She scowled, confused. "What is this, 'twiddle'?"

Holland laced his fingers together and showed her.

Now she smiled, slightly. "Still, is one life worth going to war over?"

"Sometimes, yes, it is."

"A lot of people here don't like Americans."

"I imagine there're a few Americans down here who aren't big fans of Panamanians, either."

She nodded, glancing at his canteen. He passed it over, and she took a longer drink. "Gracias."

"Sure." He watched her for a moment. "Those guys that attacked you," Holland said, "were some of the people who don't like Americans."

"Yes."

"Seems they didn't care too much about their fellow Panamanians, either."

Her eyes clouded. "No."

"So they burned you out, killed your parents, and then tried to attack you. Somehow, I don't think Americans are Panama's main problem, here."

She folded her arms and glared at him.

Holland stood and looked out the dirty window. "Doesn't matter. Look, if you want to go back home, I'm not gonna stop you. I'll just tell you that there're a lot more guys like those two out there roaming the streets. I think you'd be safer sticking with me for the moment." He turned back to face her.

Tears were rolling down her dirt-streaked face.

Holland moved over and looked down at her. "Look, I'm really sorry about your family, and your home. I can help you if you come with me, but if you don't want to do that, I get it. Either way, I can't stay here any longer. If I get caught out here alone -" He let the idea hang.

Magdalena rubbed a forearm across her eyes. "No. I'll come with you."

"Okay, then. Here's the deal. We're gonna need to move fast, so you just hang on to the back of my pack, and keep moving as long as I do. You understand?"

"I understand."

"Great. I'll get you back to the base; you'll be safe there for a while. You ready?"

In spite of the fear in her eyes, she nodded.

"Let's go, then."

Paitilla Airfield
0125 Local Time

The rescue chopper flared mere yards away from the group of SEALs huddled at the center of the runway. The combat medic was nearly in shock as they touched down. He counted at least ten people laying prone on the tarmac - four of them not moving. The uninjured men had turned the runway into an emergency Casualty Collection Point, and twenty of them were set up in a defensive perimeter around their comrades.

The medic jumped out as the helicopter settled onto the pavement, and a grim-faced SEAL ran up to him.

"How many?" the medic shouted, over the noise of the helicopter's engines.

"Four KIA," the SEAL shouted back. "Eleven wounded."

The medic nodded, following the SEAL to the group of

injured men. He was grateful to see the SEALs had already triaged the survivors, placing the most critically injured closest to the landing zone. "We can only take six at a time," he shouted.

"Got it," the SEAL said. He stuck two fingers in his mouth and let out a shrill whistle. Several other SEALs came over and started loading the worst casualties into the chopper. The medic tried to focus on getting them aboard and ready to depart, but he couldn't keep from stealing glances at the four bodies lying slightly apart from the rest. This was his first combat experience. He'd tried to prepare for seeing people get killed, but *four* killed in action in the same location?

He couldn't imagine what had happened, but he knew something had gone terribly wrong.

El Chorrillo Neighborhood

"Hold up!" Boone called out. Carl and Monty ducked into two doorways on either side of the street and waited, while Boone and the others caught up. They had started off running directly toward the church, but the growing crowds kept forcing them away. They kept running into Dingbats everywhere they turned, and every Dingbat shouted and beckoned for help when they saw the Americans. They were four blocks east of the church now, in a more industrial area. Warehouses and scrapyards were mixed with decrepit homes and small apartments, and cyclone fencing topped with razor wire criss-crossed property boundaries everywhere they looked. Boone couldn't shake the distinct sense they were being herded, driven against their will.

Now I know how a cow feels, Boone thought. *Screw that.*

"Listen up," he said as Dane and Marvin came running up. "We can't keep going this way; there's less and less cover as we get toward the beach, and too many obstacles with all these fences. We need to move back to the west."

"That's gonna put us back in contact with those Dingbats,"

Marvin pointed out.

"I get it," Boone said, watching as a car sped through an intersection two blocks away without slowing. "But we're getting boxed in here. We go much further, we'll be completely in a corner. I'd rather hole up in that church we saw. That might at least make some of these clowns think twice about shooting at us."

"I don't think they care what they shoot at, Boone." Carl looked at Mills as he spoke. "I'm guessing the Dingbats aren't quite as religiously motivated as the average Panamanian."

Mills looked up. "He's right. Most of the Dignity Battalion members are atheistic, or at least irreligious. They're Noriega's disciples - a bunch of thugs looking for some kind of legitimacy. They might hesitate to attack a church, but probably not for long."

Boone nodded. "Even so, it's the best option we have at the moment." As if to punctuate that, a group of Dingbats rounded a corner to the west and spotted them. Several of the Panamanians panicked and ducked back out of sight, but three of them started shooting. The SEALs returned fire, quickly killing all three men.

"We gotta go back west, fellas," Boone said as the gunfire faded. That church isn't far from the beach. We can hole up there for a bit; regroup before we head for the water."

"Works for me," Dane said. He had a bullet wound in his thigh that he'd managed to wrap a bandage around. The bandage was soaked with blood, but Dane didn't seem to notice. "Gonna have to fight our way back, though."

"We're gonna have to fight no matter what we do," Boone said, "so I'd just as soon choose the battlefield. The church is on a little rise, plus it looked like it's made of stone, so it gives us a defensible point on high ground." He looked at the helicopter pilot, who shook his head.

"Don't ask me," the pilot said. "We're following you guys."

Monty raised his rifle and fired three rounds as another Dingbat ran across the street. The man went down, clutching his leg, and dragged himself into an alley. "Whatever we do, we need to do it fast. These guys are sure to have friends inbound any minute now."

Boone glance around at the rest of the men, getting resigned nods all around. "All right. Let's split into two elements, four guys each side of the street." He was mostly talking for the benefit of Mills and the pilots, who had no ground combat experience. "We're gonna leapfrog the intersections two by two, one runner on each side of the street, okay? Guys running are covered by the rest of us, then the next guys go through. Stay close to the guy in line ahead of you, sing out if you start to fall behind." He dropped the half-empty magazine from his rifle and inserted a fresh one in its place, pocketing the other.

"Let's go to church."

CHAPTER SEVEN

FUBAR

El Chorrillo Neighborhood

The only indication Holland had that Magdalena was hit was a tiny squeak she let out as she fell to the pavement behind him. They were halfway through an intersection, totally exposed. Holland spun around and took a knee next to the girl, firing back the way they had come. He took two quick shots, dropping one man in the open and forcing another to duck down behind an abandoned car. He quickly slung the rifle over his right shoulder, then grabbed Magdalena and hoisted her over his left. Standing up, he steadied her with his left hand and pulled his pistol with his right, then turned and ran from the intersection to the south.

He could see a church bell tower rising above the other buildings a few blocks to his left. He figured he might be able to get help for Magdalena there; it might be a safe place to leave her while he tried to find Boone. She was groaning with each step he took, and his shoulder felt wet where her abdomen pressed against it. He had to get her off the street before she bled out. Bullets were snapping past his head, seemingly from all directions.

He dodged to his right, putting all his weight behind his right foot as he kicked in the front door of what looked like a pharmacy. Once inside, he gently lowered Magdalena to the floor and shoved the broken door closed behind him. The front of her shirt was covered in blood.

Holland carefully pulled her shirt up. There was a single hole in her ribs on the right side, eight inches above her navel. Putting one arm under her shoulders, he rolled her to one side and found a corresponding hole in her back. The bullet had gone through, probably breaking a rib or two and puncturing her liver as it went. The entry wound on her back was only bleeding slightly, but the exit wound was a different story.

Holland tore into his first aid kit and opened a packet of powdered coagulant, sprinkling it liberally in and around the hole. Then he tore open a large bandage and pressed it tight, covering the exit wound. He placed a smaller bandage against the entry wound, then wrapped everything tightly with a long strip of gauze.

"That'll have to do you for now."

The girl's eyes were clenched shut in agony, but she managed a nod. Holland peeked out the window. The street looked quiet, for the moment.

"We can't stay here," he said, looking around the pharmacy. "I'm surprised nobody's looted this place yet. It's just a matter of time." He crouched at her side. "We don't want to be here when that happens, so I'm gonna have to carry you again, okay?"

Magdalena nodded again, but even that caused her considerable pain.

"Okay." Holland took her hand and lifted her up, ducking down so she could lay across his shoulder again. "Here we go." He pulled the door open and went out into the street, going as fast as he could in the direction of the church steeple. He'd made it twenty feet when he heard Boone's garbled voice coming over his headset.

"- urch, about a mile south.. ...Carcel Modelo, request evac..."

Holland kept running. Boone was obviously calling for help, but Holland could hear nothing of the return transmission. There was nothing to be done other than keep going. Every step seemed to be an agony for Magdalena. He knew the jolting against his shoulder had to be torture, but carrying her that way allowed him to keep his handgun free, and it applied a limited amount of indirect pressure to her wound. Getting her to the rest of his team was the fastest way to get her better treatment and protection, so he pressed on. Boone was no longer talking on frequency, so he keyed his mic.

"Ballroom, Long Arm - how do you hear?"

"Good to hear you, Long Arm. We thought we might have lost ya. What's your location?"

"If you're at the big church south of the prison, I'm about a block to your northwest. I'm coming in plus one civilian, she's wounded pretty bad."

"All right, Long Arm - northwest is a bad idea; big crowd milling around the square in front of the church on that side. Can you go wide and come in from the southwest?"

Magdalena had gone limp. "Negative, Ballroom. My plus one is in critical condition. I'm coming straight in, I'd appreciate some cover, right away."

"Roger," Boone said. "We're coming out."

Holland burst into the square at a run, pistol extended to his front. As he came into the open from the narrow side street, he saw a crowd of more than fifty people milling around the square, several of them pointing at the church and arguing as if they were unsure what to do.

Beyond the crowd, the front door of the church was opening and several SEALs were streaming out. Two more came around the outside corners of the building at the same time. The crowd was turning to look at them, caught off guard and turning away from Holland and Magdalena.

"MOVE, MOVE, MOVE!!" Holland bellowed at the crowd,

not breaking stride. Several people snapped back around to look at him, startled to find another American suddenly charging at them from behind. Holland took a shot at a man with a shotgun, and Boone's men opened up at the same time, firing at anyone in the crowd holding a weapon.

The crowd panicked. Caught in a crossfire, none of them seemed to notice that half of that crossfire was coming from a lone man with a pistol, carrying an unconscious girl on his shoulder. They broke under the threat, and people were suddenly scattering in every direction. One man made the fatal mistake of running straight at Holland without dropping his AK-47. Holland shot him when they were no more than ten feet apart, and the man collapsed, falling against Holland's legs and bringing him and Magdalena to the ground in a heap.

On the church steps, Boone was picking his targets, carefully avoiding anyone who wasn't holding a weapon. The crowd was thinning rapidly, most of the people vanishing down side streets and into alleyways, and in a few moments, the square was empty. Holland was down on one knee in the middle of the square, struggling to pick up a slender Panamanian woman who was covered in blood. Boone ran down the steps to help as the rest of the team covered them. He helped Holland lift the woman off the ground, and they all retreated into the church.

A nervous looking priest met them at the front door, chattering in Spanish and making hand gestures that were less than welcoming. Boone brushed the man aside. Carl and Marvin took up positions near the door where they could watch the square, and Boone led Holland into the sanctuary.

"Put her there." Boone pointed to an open area next to the confessional. He was already tearing open a first aid kit. Holland gently laid Magdalena on the floor and checked for a pulse. He couldn't find one.

"No pulse, Boone." Holland started doing chest compressions.

Boone nodded, tearing into the med kit with new energy. He

found what he was looking for and moved to Holland's side. "Watch out, brother." Holland made room, and Boone jabbed a pen-shaped syringe into Magdalena's thigh. Holland went back to giving chest compressions, and Boone started mouth-to-mouth. Between breaths he hollered at Monty to set up a plasma IV to deal with the massive amount of blood Magdalena had lost.

Holland felt for a pulse again. This time, it was barely noticeable, but it was definitely there. Monty limped over and set up the IV while Boone verified the girl was breathing on her own again.

"Crowd's coming back, Ballroom," Carl called from the narthex at the front of the church.

"Roger that." Boone bent over Magdalena, listening closely to her breathing. "I think she's stable for the moment," he said, looking at Holland. He hadn't noticed until then that the younger man was covered in blood from his left shoulder to his waist. "You hit?"

Monty forced the IV bag into the nervous priest's hand and said something in Spanish, then moved to check on Holland.

"I don't think so," Holland said. He rocked backward on his heels and sat down hard. "Just tired."

"I bet," Boone said, grinning. "You looked like some kind of Rambo, running through that crowd with your pistol in one hand and this girl slung over your other shoulder. Until that guy tripped you, at least."

Holland managed a tired grin. He looked like something out of a nightmare - his face covered in camouflage paint, dirt and blood, with streaks through it all caused by the sweat that had poured off him during his escape; most of his upper body was a bloody mess from Magdalena's wounds. "I tried to jump over that guy," he said. "My legs just didn't want to, at that point."

"Rambo never gets tired," Monty said, prodding the priest to raise the IV a little higher. "So you must not be him."

"I'm okay with that," Holland said. "I don't think I could save the world and still find time to shave my chest."

"Jealous," Boone said. He looked intently at Holland. "You good to stay with her?"

Holland nodded. "I'm good."

"Great. Monty, let's go see what we can do about that crowd before they come back and storm this place."

Twenty minutes later, Magdalena was still unconscious, but her bleeding had stopped and she was still alive. Holland had taken turns holding her IV with the priest, who seemed finally resigned to the fact that the Americans would only leave his church when they were good and ready. Boone had finally got through to command on the radio, and now Holland could hear multiple engines rumbling outside as a group of American APCs rolled into the square. Intermittent sounds of automatic weapons fire told where parts of the crowd were being driven back by force.

Boone trotted back into the nave. "You know what George Washington said to his men before they crossed the Potomac?"

Holland looked up. "No, what?"

"He said, 'Get in the boat.'"

Holland shook his head as he helped Monty lift Magdalena onto a nylon combat stretcher. "That might be the stupidest thing I've ever heard."

"What?" Boone looked hurt. "Why? Somebody had to tell 'em to get in the boat, didn't they?"

"Maybe so," Holland said, "but that's not why it's stupid."

"Okay professor, I give up. Why is it stupid?"

"Because," Holland said, grinning slightly. "Washington and his men crossed the Delaware River, not the Potomac."

Boone laughed. "Whatever, Einstein." He pointed outside. "Just go get in the boat."

"Anything you say, Mister President." Holland took the foot of Magdalena's stretcher while Monty took the head. Outside, six U.S. Army LAV-25 eight-wheeled armored vehicles were arrayed around the front of the church, their 25 millimeter main guns aimed outward. A soldier waved Holland and Monty over, directing them to the passenger compartment in the back of one of the vehicles. They were trotting down the church steps when Holland looked down and saw Magdalena's eyes open.

"Welcome back," he said, smiling at her. "We were a little worried about you."

She had tears in her eyes, but she managed to return the smile.

Howard Air Force Base
Panama City, Panama
December 20, 1989
0230 Local Time

The LAV-25 was not the most comfortable way to travel, but under the circumstances, Holland figured it was better than walking. He'd never felt so tired in his life. He'd lost track of how many people he'd been forced to shoot at during the course of the past couple of hours, but the idea weighed on him like a boulder in his chest. He watched Magdalena, sleeping on a gurney mounted against the wall of the vehicle. Her face was ashen, but he could see she was still breathing. That made him feel only slightly better.

The APC slowed, and the vehicle commander shouted back at them. "We're coming through the gate at Howard now, fellas! We'll have you out in a couple of minutes!"

Monty shouted their thanks, then looked at Holland. "You doin' okay, Tulip?"

Holland glanced up at him. "I think so, yeah."

"Because, that was some crazy bit of escaping and evading you did tonight."

Holland looked at Monty again, trying to detect a coming joke, but the other man seemed completely serious. "Didn't really see any other way to get it done."

"Maybe not," Monty said. "But take it from me, youngster. My first action was in Grenada, and we didn't get into anything near as hairy then as we did tonight. I thought I was pretty squared away before then, but I couldn't sleep for weeks after that fight. I was a lot like you - pretty new to the team, never been in combat before, sure as hell never killed anybody before." He paused to stuff his mouth with sunflower seeds he'd produced from a pocket. "Want some?" he asked, his voice muffled.

Holland shook his head. "No, thanks."

"Anyway, what I figured out later was that you can let it get to you, or you can get past it. Now, there's a thousand ways that it can get to you; drugs, alcohol, women, gambling - any or all of those might seem like an escape, but they can all end up ruining you instead."

"So? How can you get past it, then?"

Monty couldn't resist. "Drugs, alcohol, women..."

Holland smiled and looked back across at Magdalena. Still alive.

"I'm kidding," Monty said. "Obviously, those things don't have any answers for a guy who's trying to justify doing what his country required him to do."

"What he volunteered to do," Holland interrupted.

"Yeah, that's right. We're all volunteers. But that doesn't mean we're not just as compelled to do our jobs as we would have been if we'd been pressed into service. Look at it this way. A shepherd trains a dog to protect his sheep. The dog doesn't bother to ask the wolves for permission to do his job - he just does it. He doesn't go out looking for wolves to fight either, but if they show up and start giving his flock the stink-eye, he's gonna bite, right?"

"Sure."

"Thing is," Monty paused to crack a seed and spit the hull onto the floor, "you can't train just any old mutt to be a sheep dog. Certain breeds are just better for it. Some little ratty

Chihuahua will bite anything and anyone that even startles it, including its owner, or even the sheep. A big doberman might go out and chase after anything that comes near, even if it's not a threat, and that leaves the flock vulnerable.

"But take a dog like an Anatolian Shepherd. They come from Turkey - big, smart, independent dogs - and they're ferocious when they need to be. That's us, man. We don't go looking for a fight, but if somebody starts it, we're gonna finish it - and fast, right?"

Holland just looked at him.

"*That's* how you get past it, man," Monty said. "You gotta accept that it isn't wrong to defend people from criminals and killers, even if that means the criminals and killers get hurt in the process." He leaned back in his seat and spit another shell at his feet. "You figure that out, and you'll sleep like a baby the rest of your life. Guaranteed."

The APC lurched to a sudden halt, and the rear doors slowly opened. Holland stayed in his seat, letting Monty get out first before he followed. Medics rushed into the compartment and took Magdalena out, carrying her across a wide lawn and into the base hospital. Holland watched her go, and felt a sense of satisfaction that she'd made it that far. Monty was already walking toward the other APCs, so Holland ran to catch up. He put a hand on the older man's shoulder.

"Thanks, Monty."

"No worries, brother. That's what we're here for."

They found the rest of their team spread out on the grass around the APCs. The vehicle crews were already on their way back out, after handshakes and thanks were passed all around. As Holland and Monty walked up, an Army lieutenant Holland had never seen before got out of a car and came over.

"Listen up!" he said. The men all turned to look. "The assault on Paitilla Airport was met with heavy resistance." Every man went still, and Holland had a sudden sick feeling rising in his throat as the officer went on. "The three platoons conducting the assault were ambushed by Panamanian forces under cover in the hangars at the north end of the field. Casualties were... higher than expected."

Boone was the first to speak up. "'Higher than expected?' How high is that, exactly?"

The lieutenant looked uncomfortable. "Four dead. Eleven wounded."

"Four dead?" Carl asked, shocked. "Which four? What platoon were they in?"

"That information is still being gathered at the moment. A full briefing will be held as soon as we have all the details."

"That assault plan was an Army FUBAR from the start," Monty growled.

The officer was hurriedly trying to change the subject. "You men who are hurt, go get yourselves looked at; the rest of you, get some rest."

"Hey, jackass, every one of us is hurt," Monty snapped. Boone laid a hand on his chest and whispered something to him, and Monty stopped talking.

The officer tried to placate them. "I understand you're upset -"

Boone turned on him. "All due respect, sir, but you're just talking your way into a deeper hole. I'm guessing somebody chose you to tell us this because you were the lowest ranking officer in the room. That's a raw deal, but having a stranger who doesn't look like he's ever gotten his uniform dirty stand here and tell us that he understands how we feel about four of our friends getting killed because of some Army officer's messed up plan - that's way worse." He stepped closer, lowering his voice. "You did what you were told to do, lieutenant. You'd do well to just leave us to our own, now."

The lieutenant opened his mouth, but nothing came out. Embarrassed, he turned, got back in his car and drove off.

With the Army officer gone, the SEALs had nowhere to direct their anger, and it quickly morphed into stunned resignation as they all reluctantly started to shuffle toward the hospital. Mills, the rescued civilian, had gone unnoticed by the Army lieutenant. Dressed in a SEAL helmet and body armor, he'd blended in enough that in the moment of grief, they'd all forgotten that he was the reason they hadn't been at Paitilla that night. Now he trotted to catch up with Boone.

"I need to thank you guys," he said. "For getting me out."

Boone looked at him, then nodded. "No problem, man. We were just doing our jobs." His jaw tightened. "At least something went right tonight."

"I'm real sorry about your friends, too."

Boone nodded. "Thanks. So am I."

"I don't want to sound stupid, but can I ask - what Monty said to that lieutenant - what's FUBAR?"

Boone stopped and turned to face Mills as the rest of the team filed past them through the sliding hospital doors. "It means, 'fouled up beyond all recognition'." He slapped Mills lightly on the shoulder, then turned and went inside.

Air Force Clinic
Howard Air Force Base, Panama
December 25, 1989

"How are you feeling?" Holland leaned through the open doorway. Magdalena was propped up in the hospital bed with several tubes in her arm. She had dark circles under her eyes, but otherwise she looked healthy.

"Ola," she said. She looked at the scraggly bouquet of flowers Holland was carrying and smiled. "You didn't bring those for me, did you?"

He fidgeted, embarrassed that he hadn't found something better. "They're not much. Just thought you could use something to brighten this place up."

"They're pretty. Gracias."

Holland carefully set the little vase on the side table and pulled up a chair. "I'm sorry you have to spend Christmas in the hospital."

"I don't mind," she said. "If not for you and your friends, I'd be spending it in a graveyard." She smiled. "This is better."

Holland nodded, looking around the spartan room. He was uncomfortable, and it showed.

"Will you return home soon?" she asked. "To America?"

"Yeah. Supposed to fly out tonight, actually. I wanted to check on you before I left, I guess. Make sure you were doing okay."

"The doctor, he said you saved my life." Her eyes were bright, but she was still smiling. "He said if you hadn't bandaged my wound, I would have bled to death. Thank you."

"I should have been there sooner," Holland said.

"If you had, then maybe our paths would not have crossed." She reached out her hand, and Holland took it. "You were there, because God put you there, Lawson. He put you there so you could save me."

"If He'd put me there earlier, I might have saved your family, too."

"You don't know that." She squeezed his hand. "Listen to me. You're not to blame for my parents' deaths. But you *did* save my life, and I am grateful for that."

He let go of her hand, clearly uncomfortable with accepting gratitude for something he saw as a failure. "What will you do now? I mean," he waved an arm at the room, "when you get out of here?"

"My aunt and uncle live in Colón," she said, "at the other end of the canal. I'm told there was some fighting there also, but not as bad as it was here. I'll try to contact them, I think."

Holland lowered his eyes. "I'm really sorry about your parents, Magdalena."

"I know, and thank you. I like to think they're in heaven now."

Holland didn't know quite how to respond to that.

"I've been thinking about it a great deal, you know."

"About what? Heaven?"

"Mm, yes, some. But more about life. I understand now how short it really is, and how quickly it can end."

Holland nodded, content to just let her talk.

"That helped me to appreciate all I have in life."

His eyebrows went up. "But - you lost everything!"

"Not everything," she said. "Before you saved me, I thought my life would always be the same - living with my parents, working in their bodega. Maybe I'd get married someday; but I knew I would never leave my barrio. My parents were very protective of me. They discouraged me from leaving, because they were afraid to leave. They were afraid of many things, but mostly anything outside the barrio. They said the world was dangerous. So they stayed in their bodega while their neighborhood got worse and worse, and then what they were hiding from found them anyway."

"That's a shame."

"It is, but I realized that I can learn from that. Because I almost lost my life, now I don't want to waste any more of it. I want to live it. When my life does finally end someday, I don't want to have regrets. I don't want to spend my life hiding in fear, like my parents. Fear can only hurt you if you let it - and they did."

Holland stared at her, and it felt as if something that had been eating at him for months now suddenly made sense. "I think maybe I should be thanking you, Magdalena."

"I don't understand."

"You just helped me to see that I've been hiding from something, too."

She laughed. "I cannot imagine you hiding from anything."

Holland stood. "I guess we all have things we're scared of. But you just taught me that fear is a choice."

"So? What will you choose to do?"

"Same as you," he said, taking her hand and squeezing it. "I'm gonna stop hiding."

She smiled, her face lighting up. "I'm glad. Thank you for the flowers, and thank you again for all you did."

"Happy to help, Magdalena. Merry Christmas." He gave her hand a final squeeze, and walked out of the room.

He almost ran over Boone, who was just about to enter. Holland looked down and noticed that Boone was carrying an even more pathetic bouquet than the one he'd brought. He arched an eyebrow.

"What?" Boone said. "It's not cool that she's in here, all alone, on Christmas. She might like some company, that's all."

Holland grinned, and stepped aside. "Merry Christmas, Boone."

CHAPTER EIGHT

Epilogue

Little Creek, Virginia
January 1990

Holland and Boone sat in silence in the team room. The four empty gear cages stuck out amid the rows of full ones like missing teeth in an otherwise perfect smile. Holland couldn't stop himself from glancing at them as he stuffed some personal items in a bag.

"Two weeks," Boone said, breaking the uncomfortable silence.

Holland nodded, and kept packing.

"Not a lot of time to grieve." Boone was leaning forward in his chair with his elbows on his knees, looking up at Holland with barely concealed worry.

"No, it isn't," Holland finally said. 'But that's all the leave they're giving us."

"Mm-hmm." Boone looked at the floor. "So. Where you gonna spend it?"

Holland zipped his bag shut and stood up, glancing around one last time at the four empty cages.

"With a friend," he said. "Fixing a mistake."

"Did you call this 'friend', first?"

"Nope."

"That's a mistake, brother."

"No, it isn't," Holland said. "I don't want to say what I have to say over the phone, that's all. Now that we're all done with our debriefings and after-action reviews, I finally have a chance to say it in person. So I'm going down there, to say it in person."

"First thing she's gonna say is, 'How come you didn't call?'"

"Tell you what," Holland said, heading for the door. "If that's the first thing she says, I'll buy you a beer."

"You already owe me a beer!" Boone called after him, but the door was already slamming shut.

Port Royal, Jamaica
The Next Day

The bar was packed with vacationers, and Lexie was running between tables, trying to keep up with the demand. Holland could see her from the beach as she bustled back and forth, but he couldn't make his feet carry him closer. People flowed around him like water around a rock. He was about to give up and walk away when Lexie looked up, saw him, and froze.

He thought he should wave, or smile, or something, but it was all he could do to just stay put. He knew she must hate him for the way he'd pushed her away, and he wasn't entirely sure what he'd expected by traveling down here, but if nothing else, he thought he at least owed her an apology face to face. So he held his ground and waited as she waved another waitress over, then walked out of the bar and across the sand toward him.

He watched her come, dreading the insults she would no doubt be eager to heap on him, and knowing he deserved them all. He could see the pain on her face, the anger and the hurt. Knowing he'd caused all that made him feel disgusted with himself, and as Lexie stopped in front of him, he knew he couldn't blame her for anything she could possibly be prepared to say.

Which was why he was caught flat footed by what she *did* say.

"Are you okay?"

He blinked. "Me?"

She knotted her brows. "Who'd you think I was asking? You look like you're hurting, and there's no one else standing here."

He was at a complete loss. Insults, anger, tears - he thought he'd prepared for every possibility, but compassion? Toward *him?*

"I... I thought you'd be the one who was hurting, Lexie. I didn't expect you to be worried about me."

"So, you came all the way down here to 'protect' me from hurt?"

Holland thought he detected a hint of sarcasm, but the half smile on Lexie's face betrayed her. He gave a sheepish looking grin. "I'm a pretty big idiot, aren't I?"

She shrugged. "You're an average sized idiot, with great expectations."

He smiled for a moment, then frowned again. "Saying 'I'm sorry' doesn't come close to how I really feel, Lexie."

"I know."

"I think pushing you away was the biggest mistake of my life." He looked at his feet. "I just wanted you to know that. Wanted to tell you in person."

"Do you still believe what you said?"

"Which part?"

"That it's not fair to expect me to have a relationship with someone like you?"

"Honestly? I'm not sure about anything any more." He looked at her. "I think my wanting to be with you, knowing what that might put you through - it's selfish." She watched him, letting him sink or swim. "It's selfish," he said again, "but what's worse than that, is that I don't care."

"Don't care about what, exactly?"

"I know being with me won't be easy for you, but I can't help it - I still want to be with you."

"You realize - that doesn't mean that you don't care, Lawson. It means that you *do*."

He scratched his head and looked at his feet again. "Well, I guess that's something, then." He looked past her shoulder to the busy bar. "I should let you get back to work. Thanks, Lexie - for hearing me out."

She almost laughed. "So you came all this way to say that, and now you're going to walk away again? You really *are* terrible at romance, you know that?"

Holland looked thoroughly confused. "I... I just thought... maybe you'd be with someone else by now."

"Oh, I am," she said, deadpan. Holland's face fell. "I married a billionaire and moved to the south of France. We have two kids and we're insanely happy, which is why I still commute to Jamaica to work in my brother's grubby little bar."

He couldn't help smiling now. "You're right. I'm terrible at romance."

"I think I can forgive you for that," she said. "I'm off work in three hours. Come back then, and you can practice sweeping me off my feet."

"I probably can't give you a house in the south of France, no matter how much I practice."

"That's no problem." She turned and started back to the bar, looking back at him over her shoulder. "France is overrated. Just like romance."

They were married three days later.

About the Author

M.P. MacDougall is an American historian and author of thrillers, humorous satire and fantasy. The youngest of twelve children, he grew up on a suburban farm, spending much of his free time chasing cows, perfecting bicycle stunts and playing in the dirt, and he never had to wear a helmet or use anti-bacterial soap. He was a professional Air Traffic Controller for more than twenty-six years, and a practitioner of the art of sarcastic banter and snide commentary for much longer than that. He holds a Bachelor of Arts in World Military History, because he's afraid he'll lose it if he puts it down. He lives with his very patient wife and kids in the Pacific Northwest of the United States.

Also By M.P. MacDougall

Lawson Holland Thrillers
    The Blood of Tyrants
    The Blood of Patriots
    The Tree of Liberty
    Sing Your Death Song - Coming Soon!

How To Steer Your Kid Series (Humor/Satire)
    Jet Screamer
    Meat Sandwiches

Harvey Bennett Prequels (With Nick Thacker)
    The Icarus Effect

Learn more about the author at
MPMacDougall.com

Thanks so much for reading!